LIB
WITHDRA

GLIMPSES OF SKY

Sky water. It needs no fence. Nations come and go without defiling it. It is a mirror which no stone can crack; whose quicksilver will never wear off, whose gilding Nature continually repairs; no storms, no dust can dim its surface ever fresh; a mirror in which all impurity presented to it sinks, swept and dusted by the sun's hazy brush, this is the light dust cloth, which retains no breath that is breathed on it, but sends its own to float as clouds high above its surface, and be reflected in its bosom still.

Chapter 1: Leaving home

Heaven is under our feet as well as over our heads

"Hurry up, Martha, he's waiting!"

Martha remained as she was, small knees pressed into warped floorboards, lips moving in silent prayer.

"Martha! Will you come on!"

The hearer, normally compliant, was slow today. She took one final look around the crammed room she shared with her two sisters and three brothers since she was a baby. This was where she nursed them when

4

they were sick, and rocked them when they were afraid. Most of the time, it was a crowded, noisy place to be, but, thanks to Martha, it was never untidy. Thanks to Martha, nobody ever went angry to their rickety bed at night. She said their prayers with them every morning, got the youngest ones dressed, and did their school work with them in the afternoons. As the eldest, these were only some of her jobs, but she did them all gladly. Even though as the second eldest her brother Peter would have been more than able to do his fair share, their father had claimed him for the neighbouring farm he worked on, and that was that.

Scraping a seatless chair beneath the single, stingy window, the 17 year old girl put one foot on either side of the frame, and standing on tiptoe, looked out.

She let her gaze run along the grey slated roof, over the almost leafless trees, across the serene forest-lined estuary, and lastly rest at the sea. The wind was picking up, and she followed the rolling cloud shadows over the hills, pulling her back to the chipped blue window-frame, the wobbling chair, the busy room, the insistent shouts of her mother. She wouldn't try to see her heart's home again, but knew she would always carry it with her.

"Martha!"
"I'm coming, mammy"

Martha lifted up a bundle wrapped in used brown paper, creaked across the uneven roof-space, ran down the wired wooden ramp, and around the outside steps to the front door. Opening the bottom half, she moved into a dark space, lit by a small window of sun, and a meagre peat fire. The man sitting by it knocked his pipe on the stone flags and stood up, gruff.

"Martha, at last. We're so sorry, Father, for keeping you waiting. I hope you enjoyed your tea?"

Martha's mother was flapping and hotly flustered. She did not have the time, in her family- filled existence, to entertain a priest. But her staunch Catholicism would never allow her to say so. Martha's pending new life was a necessity - they didn't have the means to keep her at home. It was time she made a place for herself elsewhere.

"Well now, are you ready, Martha?"

Father Francis waved his stick in the direction of the door.

"Yes, Father." Martha whispered her reply, and shifted her luggage from one hand to the other. She kissed her mother. Her other brothers and sisters stopped collecting kindling to wave as she walked up the steep path through the pine woods. She paused at the gate, resting her fingers on it for a moment, remembering the day her father made it. The bolt slid open easily, and then, she was out, beyond the shelter of the trees, and at the mercy of a northerly wind.

There was a horse and trap waiting, restless.

"Right-o, here we are now, up you get,"

The priest climbed up and waited for Martha. She struggled up, parcel first, and with a crack, they set off over the potholed road.

"I suppose I'd better tell you where we're headed now Martha."

Breath held, she gripped her seat, and

waited.

"It's a wee way away, but not too far you couldn't get back if they were ever to give you a day off. There's no sea-view like you're used to, but there are trees. Plenty."

Martha looked away, as the priest went on.

"Listen, dear, there's nothing to be afraid of. You've got your prayers to help you, and your faith to keep you. You can't be asking many questions when you're there, or speaking much at all - it'll serve you better if you keep quiet, and let things take their course. She's a God-fearing lady. That's all that matters anyway."

Martha nodded, serious. Even more terrified now she knew where she was going. Who she was going to.

The bumpy road and grim silence stretched on. Eventually, they turned into a smoother path, and stopped. Facing the trap is a dark tunnel, a tunnel leading to what was always a mysterious place to Martha and her family. Father Francis crossed himself before he urged his horse into the black. Martha strained to see light in the distance, but the forest had swallowed it.

An eternity held in seconds later, they emerged and made their way through thin, towering trees and ancient moss-covered stones. The forest was whispering, the wind crying through the high branches. There were no inhabitants to be seen. Eventually, they broke into a clearing.

"There it is. Your new home."

Shaking, Martha looked down into the valley, and saw a huge, grey, dark-windowed dwelling. The trees had been cleared around it, leaving a barren space. A red-brick barricade lined one side of the lane. There was no garden, that she could see, but, about half-way along the wall, there was a door that made her wonder.

They made their uneasy way down to the front drive. Father Francis was whistling under his breath. Wee Martha used her finger-tips to Hail Mary herself into calmness.

"Right-ho, down we get, Martha."

Priest and girl climbed down, passed the overwhelming front entrance and walked round the side of the house to the kitchen door. He raised his stick and banged on the wood. A moment passed. Martha could hear the racket of saucepans, dishes, hissing water and shouting servants. He tried again. The door was pulled open.

"Alright, alright, calm yoursel, for God's - oh! Father Francis!"

The round woman flustered, caught. Father Francis gave her a pacifying hand raise.

"Good morning to you Betty. This is Martha, the new maid. Why don't you take me up to Lady Fitzgerald, and then show the girl where she's to be."

"Yes, yes, of course, Father." Betty squinted at Martha, and led them both inside.

The group moved through the house, along a shabby-grand corridor with frowning portraits, and into a dimly-lit, long and narrow room. At the end of it, Martha could just make out the figure of a woman, sitting beside the only lamp, motionless. Martha found herself in the second dark tunnel of the day.

"Who is this, Betty?" The mistress strained to see.

Father Francis stepped forward, and gestured for Martha to approach.

"Good day to you, Lady Fitzgerald. I've brought a new maid for your approval."

"Good day. Let's see you then." Lady Fitzgerald lifted Martha's chin to scrutinise her face, and then did a full, veterinarian examination of her hands, arms, legs and feet. Martha made her own observations; seeing a fragile woman, with a hardness to her features that made her almost inscrutable. She was dressed all in black, with no relief of light or colour, blending in to the darkness around her. Catching herself staring, Martha looked down.

"Seems healthy. Bit small. Good worker's hands. Have you anything to say, child?"

"Thank-you for the opportunity, ma'am. I will do my best to deserve it." Martha spoke in a quiet voice, but lifted her eyes to show her sincerity.

"Well. I shall be the judge of that. You will do what you're told, never speak unless bidden, and never, ever stray beyond the boundaries of my woods, without my particular permission. Is that clear?"

Martha nodded, heart breaking, and turned to follow Betty to her new sleeping quarters. "You're in the attic. Room to yourself."

They climbed narrow steps and crouched into Martha's bedroom, more like a cupboard with a bed stuffed in. Martha took everything in without having to turn her head: the lumpy, short mattress, the cracked wash-bowl and jug beside it, about 12 inches of chipped wooden floor at the foot of the bed and another hard-to-reach, narrow window. Because of its height, there was no way of telling what was outside it, but the dark wall beneath it broke with light, which was all that really mattered.

"I wonder if it would be possible to have a

chair?"

"What a funny thing to ask for. Sure you'll hardly be here, and when you are, you'll be sleeping. Ach, now, don't be looking like that. I'll ask Danny if there's any lying about. Can't promise nothing though."

Betty puffed downstairs, muttering. Martha slowly unpacked her bundle, then, realising there was nowhere to put her few possessions, repacked. Stretching her arms out, she touched two walls and closed her eyes in an attempt to conjure up a wider space. Then, she knelt down and prayed for a chair.

"You'll not find much hope down there, m'dear."

Someone was poking his head through the door. His stunted frame fitted through, his few remaining teeth leading the way. Martha pulled herself up. Eyes sparkling through folds of aged skin were looking at her. Something was tapping on the floor, and her visitor was smiling.

"You asked for a chair, madam?"

Martha felt tears rising, and clasped her hands together.

"Oh! That was quick.   I didn't know whether they'd have any - but I'm so glad they did - life without a view wouldn't be worth anything. You must be Danny?"

"That's what they tell me. Let's see if this works. Best to climb up, not bend down, I always say."

Together, Martha and Danny awkwardly hauled the old seat into her room, and both moved, without question, beneath the window. He held out his hand, she gripped it, and stepped up.

Seconds of silence ticked past.

"Well, can you see it?"

"See what?"

"You know."

"The sky. I can see the sky!"

"There we are then. Any sea?"

Martha stepped down, shaking her head,

14

puzzled.

"How could I find that here? There's only trees, I've been told." Martha tried not to sigh.

"Don't believe them. There's more to this place than you think. Secret wonders, all over the estate. Maybe, some day, I'll show you some of them."

Martha climbed down, heart lifted. Perhaps this place would not be so dark after all.

Chapter 2: The bird

(Birds) give me a new sense of variety and capacity of that nature which is our common dwelling.

The first days struggled past in a stifling drudge of chores, unfamiliar faces, and narrow corridors. Each night Martha lay down in darkness, and each morning, she prayed in the shadows - looking up to the black square, wishing it was blue. She hadn't seen Danny since that first day, his work enviably taking him outside, while hers shut her in. The other maids were civil, but harried, and would take more work than Martha had the stamina to give.

For the first time in her life, she noticed a need within herself that had never mattered before. She realised she was rarely alone, or still, in her family home- there were always little ones to supervise, cooking and cleaning to be done, or chores outside in the woods. Life was busy here too, but it was strangely silent. Betty had obviously decided that Martha was not a talker, and had given her jobs that could be achieved in isolation. She had misjudged her, perhaps, not realising that prayerfulness and timidity do not always mean a desire for solitude. Martha missed her noisy brothers and sisters, and missed being thanked for her work, as her mother had always made sure to do. There was no way of knowing whether she'd spent too long brushing the bedroom floors, or beating out the rugs, or dusting the mantelpieces, because she worked by herself. Sometimes she sang quietly, or watched the movement of trees, birds and sky outside the window, but other times, she just looked down and worked mechanically.

One morning, she was cleaning the hearth in one of the bedrooms. It was a stifling day outside, and suffocating in. Glancing over her shoulder towards the open door, she moved over to the window, and lifted the sash. Fresh air rushed in, and she stopped to greet it. It moved around her, giving her freedom to breathe without struggle, cooling her flushed cheeks and pushing her fine brown hair back from her face. Turning back to the soot, she heard a new sound. A flapping, cheeping sound. It went above her, around her, and out through the door into the corridor beyond. Martha ran to follow, but a scream stopped her. Seconds passed, and with the screams and the flapping building, she moved towards them. She found herself at the entrance to another, grander room. There, standing shrieking on a chair with the blackbird frantic around her, was her mistress.

"Get it away! Beast! Get away from me!"

Martha walked past the frenzy, and opened a window. Wide.

"What are you doing? How dare you! You will kill me with this air! How dare you!"

Lady Fitzgerald was now grovelling around the floor, one hand shielding her face from the bird, one holding her skirts over her mouth.

The trapped creature, seeing the air and the light, flew towards it, and was free. Martha pulled the window shut again. The mistress, retreating into shadows, took several deep breaths.

"I am sorry, ma'am. He's away now, you are safe."

Martha got down beside the shaking woman, and touched her hand. She met her wide eyes, and for a whisper of a moment, saw gratitude.

"Can I get you anything, ma'am?"

When there was no answer, the little servant backed out of the room, turned and headed back to work, marvelling at the height of hysteria a little bird had induced in her mistress, as though she'd never encountered one before. Surely this lady knew a bit of nature, having lived so closely surrounded by it for years. If she feared it so much, why did she stay, and not move to the town house she's bound to own. Martha let herself entertain these wonderings as she moved the brush over the grate, and pushed the ashes down into the darkness beneath.

Chapter 3: Eating in company

I never found the companion that was so companionable as solitude.

It was November, and the house had already endured two merciless winter storms. There had been a fair number of trees down, and slates off the roof. Martha's room was even colder, as the freezing gales pushed through cold walls, and rattled the high window incessantly. She'd managed to get a second blanket, and lay curled up in a tight ball, with all the clothes she owned on. Even after a strenuous day, it was difficult to sleep, and nigh on impossible to get up and into the cold air, or wash with icy water. Not that

Martha wasn't used to low temperatures, but she'd always had plenty of warm bodies around her before, and a fire to go down to. She dreamt of the fire a lot, and often speculated whether anyone would notice if she slept on the floor in one of the many bedrooms, in front of the glowing embers of one of the many fires inexplicably lit every day. But she had never dared, and knew she never would.

After shivering her way out of bed, and grabbing her meagre breakfast from the warmth of the kitchen, Martha turned round to see Danny, chomping on his own bread roll, and smiling at her.

"I've noticed, me dear, that you never eat with the rest. I know you like to be alone, but maybe you should try eating with the other staff. Sometimes, it's good to be with people, and show them you're not unfriendly. So, give it a go. You might even like it."

Danny winked and nodded away, leaving Martha bothered. Now she'd have to do it. She knew she would. Another guilt-led decision to dread. Usually, Martha would get her food in the kitchen, bi-pass the adjoining room where the servants dined, and find a

peaceful place to enjoy it. On rainy days, she
went up to her room. On sunny days, she
found a flat stone on the low wall running
round the drive. After a life of clamouring
brothers and sisters, and having to feed each
one, this, to Martha, was bliss.

Still, the next day, she found herself
walking with slow steps towards the side-
room. The door swung open in front of her,
and the muffled voices exploded into a
battery of noise. She clutched her tin plate,
and looked around for a spare seat.
Everyone was talking to everybody else.
Even Danny. After what seemed like hours
of awkwardness, she half-sat at the end of
one of the two wooden benches, squeezed
her plate onto the table, and began to eat,
eyes down.

No-one noticed her, or her plate, and bit
by bit, both were nudged out of their place.
Martha edged away as far as she could,
hidden by a turned back, and the chatter. As
her neighbour leant against her, she moved
along. Then it happened. No space was left
for her, or her plate, and simultaneously,
both crashed to the floor. There was a now
unwelcome moment of silence. Everyone
was staring at her now, mouths twitching

with laughter, as Martha pushed herself up, gathered her ruined lunch and tried to hide her tears. Entertainment over, she was invisible again, and made her way out of the room, wishing she had never been in it, duty or not.

Chapter 4: Going to church

Let him step to the music that he hears, however measured or far away.

"Well, you must have done something. Wrong or right, it's hard to say, but the mistress wants you to accompany her this morning. To the church. Best find a fresh smock."

Betty was flustered, as ever. Martha rose from her usual early morning prayers, and looked down at her grey uniform, the only one she had.

"Where would I find one, Betty? How

long do I have?"

"There are more in the basement press. You've time yet - and don't be changing before you've finished your morning chores for me. This trip out will not put you behind on my books. Tis ridiculous, if you ask me, but no-one ever thinks to ask old Betty, oh no, what would she know? A lot, and if more listened to me, t'would be a better life for them. But that they'll never know, more fool them."

Martha watched the tirade, racing over all she had to do, and fighting the urge to edge back - though close walls helped keep her still. Once silence released her, and Betty was gone, she took a breath, then steeled herself for the flurry to come.

Chores finished, clean smock on, Martha waited at the servants' exit for the carriage.

"You look smart this morning, Martha. I hear she's wanting you this time."
Danny walked over the drive, smiling at her.

"Oh Danny, hello. Have you ever gone with her? What's it like?"

"Me? Well I do take her, but I've never gone in. I'm the driver, see. You, I warn you, won't see anything though. You'll be wishing you were up at the front with me. There'll be nothing, only sounds. Be clever, and you might get a wee look at something. But that's all it'll be, a wee look. You just remember to look within yourself, and it'll be grand."

Danny patted Martha on the shoulder, and then left her to harness up. She stood on the step, head bowed, hands clasped, waiting. Then she saw Danny again, high at the front of a faded black, windowless carriage. He jumped down, and opened one of the doors, beckoning her over. As he helped her up, he whispered "Courage" to her, and then closed the door.

Inside, it took Martha a moment to make out her mistress, but not as long as before. She was getting better at picking out the dark silhouette. She wondered how she was to curtsey, or what she was to say, but when there was no acknowledgement of her presence, she did nothing. As her eyes grew accustomed to the shadowy space, she took in the dusty, faded seats, the slatted floor, the lines where the windows had been removed, the laced edge of Lady Fitzgerald's dress, her stiff, buttoned boots. Martha looked down at her own drab appearance for a moment, and then, lifted her thoughts to the lilies of the field, the wild flowers tucked in like secret jewels amongst the woods around her home. She smiled.

"What, on earth, is there to smile about, girl?"

Martha started at the voice, and its bitterness.

"I'm sorry, ma'am. I was just thinking of God's creation, and its colours."

"How ridiculous. I try not to think. You should practice that."

The mistress signed off, turning her head towards the non-existent window. Martha couldn't help but wonder if the label of ridiculous had been wrongly assigned. She watched the tiny slits in the floor flicker, blur, and finally, freeze. She heard Danny halting the horses, and crunch over gravel to the door. Then, light, air, and her friend's solemn face. He helped Lady Fitzgerald down, but when Martha moved to follow, held his hand up. She sat back down, feeling rebuffed. He came back, though.

"She goes to visit the grave first. Then, you can get out. I'll leave the door open for you."

"Whose..." Martha stopped her curiosity and leaned across the seat to watch. The lady, only in the fourth decade of her life, looked twice that as she crossed the uneven grass of the graveyard. She never looked up, just struggled from one lump of turf to another. When she stopped at the polished granite stone, she bent down even further, paused, and then turned to come back. Something about her posture betrayed a hidden grief that made Martha's heart heavy.

"Right, now you can go. Remember, it's not what you're used to."

Danny helped her down, and she walked quickly behind her mistress, glancing once to take in the mountain on her left, and the sea, oh, the sea! on her right. The church bell was ringing, people were going in, chatting. Even that sound was welcome to Martha's ears. When they got inside, a man led them both quickly into a separate space. Martha caught herself about to genuflect, when she saw that the lady had walked straight in. She looked around - another dark box - the wooden pew was cushioned in red, but surrounded on all four sides with tall, heavy oak panels. Seeing a lower, uncushioned seat, the servant followed her mistress's lead, and sat down. She looked across from her feet, but there was nowhere for her to kneel. "How am I to pray?" she wondered. She knew this was not a church of her own Roman Catholic tradition, but she had never been in one like it.

She realised that Danny was right, she wasn't used to this - to the strange hymns, the few prayers, the absence of communion. Of course, she couldn't see anything, and was guided only by the grand, darkly clothed lady - her sole companion. After about an hour, the man, not a priest, but she didn't know what to call him, stopped with an "Amen" and then, from the clamour, she knew the service was over. She rose, expecting to leave, but Lady Fitzgerald remained seated. Following an age of confusion, when the noises had faded, they stood up and were ushered out of the pew, through a deserted church and back into the carriage.

"Still thinking of creation now?"

Martha shook her head, dutiful again. "Is this what I am called to?" she prayed. "Is this all?" The blackness seeped into her, and she had to close her eyes to find light.

Chapter 5: Christmas Eve

If a man does not keep pace with his companions, perhaps it is because he hears a different drummer.

The days passed through a grey haze, freezing into deep winter. Martha worked, prayed and reminisced herself into preserved brightness, hoping for better times. None of the household staff bothered with her, all too set in their ways to accommodate somebody new. None, that is, except Danny. Every time he passed her, in the kitchen, or out in the yard when she was hanging out the laundry to dry, or rugs and curtains for beating, he would stop for a short chat, and leave her with a word of encouragement, like 'keep it up with your praying', or 'it won't be long til spring', or 'seen anything interesting through that wee window of yours'. In these moments, Martha was lifted, and always gave back as much hope as she'd received. They were becoming good friends, despite the fact that he was an ageing man, and she a young girl. These differences didn't seem to matter, when it came to their kindred spirits. Each helped the other, without them even knowing it.

There was also silence from the top of the house, as Lady Fitzgerald went into an eery kind of hibernation, pining for something, or someone. Martha, too, longed for her family, and her home, but never dared to ask when she might see them again.

"Martha! What kind of a trance are you in?! I have news for you."

Betty, ever sentimental, snapped her fingers into Martha's thoughts, panting with the exertion of too many stairs, and too many pies perhaps.

"You're to go back to your house for Christmas Eve. Wait - don't get yourself too excited now. You're to be back here for the day after. Mistress wants a full dinner prepared. Dear knows why, there's no-one to come and eat it. But mine's not to wonder at her odd ways." Betty shook her head, and squinted at Martha.

"Thank-you, Betty, I will ask somebody to send word."

"No need, Danny, the fool, has already set out to do that for you, as if he's not needed here." Martha waited until Betty had stomped down to the first floor, and then danced a wee jig. She was going back home at last, and everything until then could be borne. She would hardly notice all the repetitive cleaning, the freezing nights, the lack of friends now. Home was getting close!

December passed with anticipation and business, and finally Martha's one precious day arrived. She'd collected some of the left-over baking from the kitchen, and retrieved the flowers she'd pressed between two stones weeks before. That was all she had to take with her. Less than she would have parcelled up from nature's abundance around her home.

Danny was driving her. No miserable priest this time, just her soul's one friend here.

"I have something for you" he said, as they drew close to the end of her lane.

"Close your eyes, and put out your hand."

Martha looked puzzled, but did as she was told, taking off one of her gloves and cupping her fingers. She felt something being dropped into them.

"You can look now."

Martha looked down, and there in her palm was a chain of small, hardened seeds, bursting with all the colours of the forest, twined together expertly, beautifully.

"Oh Danny, this is too lovely. I had no idea all these berries could be found in that forest, and they kept their colours so well. I don't know what to say, and I've nothing to give you."

"You've given me plenty, without your knowing it."

Danny cleared his throat and busied
34

himself with the reins.

"It could be said, well, I'll try to say it... It could be said that your life to me, Martha, is all colour in a dark place."

Martha's eyes filled. She pressed Danny's hand, wondering at how his arthritic fingers had managed such delicate work, and how many painful hours he had given to its making. Whispering her thanks, she got down and hurried towards her home, determined to savour the one meagre day her mistress had granted her.

"You know you've no excuse now for missing prayers. Them's rosary beads!" Danny laughed, and cracked his whip for the big house.

Christmas Eve at Martha's home was chaotic but joyful. Her father came back from the farm, and sat on his chair, smiling at his eldest daughter, glad to have his family round him. Her mother hugged her, many times over. Her brothers and sisters flung themselves at her as if she'd never left, shouting over each other with their news of loose teeth, cut knees, different school teachers, new-found games. All except the oldest one, who lifted his arms around her for a split second, and then walked, head down, towards the door. After it had banged behind him, Martha turned to face her parents. Everyone had stopped talking, and stood looking at the stone floor - the youngest ones not understanding, but sensing the heaviness and staying silent.

"What has happened to Peter?"

"He wants to go and fight, but Father won't allow it."

The words rushed out of her sister's mouth, to fill the heavy silence.

"He is not of age. And that's all we'll say of it. No more on this day, you hear? This is Martha's day."

Her father's smile had gone, and years had piled on his face. Her mother stood up, and started scrubbing an already clean work-bench.

"Fight? Where? Why would he?"

Martha's confusion gripped her throat like iron fingers, but her family did not answer.

With newly learned patience and stifled curiosity, she handed out her presents and set to making the dinner. The children, as ever, made a rapid recovery, and fell back into noisy cheer. Her parents were slower, and even when they managed to feign lightness of heart, Martha still sensed their pain.

After the meal of griddle bread and stew, and when all her siblings bar Peter were stowed away, Martha went out in the cold to look for her brother. He was standing on top of the hill, looking out at the clear night, the sea black silver below him.

Martha picked her way up the familiar path, feeling the whin bushes scraping against her legs, remembering where the easiest slabs of grey rock were, stepping over the muddiest parts, and not looking ahead or back until she stood beside him.

"I have missed this hill, and the view. Remember in the lighter evenings, when we all used to climb up, find a ledge to sit on, and wait for daddy to come home? I've missed you and the others more than any of this, Peter. It seems I have missed a lot.

Especially of you."

Peter kicked the bare stumps of blackened heather and brown bracken, sullen.

"Is there a war?"

Her brother snorted, then, sorry, patted her shoulder, as though she were the younger.

"A terrible war, Martha. A war that needs fighting. A war that I need to fight in."

Peter raised his chin up, a look of determination and conviction on his face. All of a sudden, he looked like a man, but his eyes were still young. He was pretending he knew much of the troubles of the world, but his understanding was limited. How Martha wished that he would never lose this innocence or be confronted by violence and pain, but she knew that he was hurtling head-first towards it. She was wise enough to remain silent, to know that the case had already been made, however much she was tempted to make it again. So she just stood beside him, and let the night fill the silence.

"Happy Christmas, Peter."

Chapter 6: The Christmas dinner

Our vision does not penetrate the surface of things

The morning rushed in all too quickly, and there she was again, taking her final hasty sweep of the view and saying her goodbyes. She had hugged Peter, and felt the tears rising, but knew he'd want her to show courage. That strength of character was the one thing that was pushing him towards what he felt was his duty, in the same way that Martha always followed hers. Her parents were brusque, as they knew this parting was necessary and unavoidable. They couldn't afford to keep their eldest daughter at home, no matter how many of the household burdens she would carry for them.

Once again, she found herself standing waiting at the end of the lane for the cart to take her back. This time was not any less painful than the first, but the fear had gone, replaced with sinking dread. She did not know when Lady Fitzgerald's whims would bend favourably towards her. She did not know when she would be home again. All she knew was her duty.

Danny sensed Martha's need for silence, and they spoke little on the journey back. As they pulled away, she'd turned to look back and saw Peter standing on the hill, hands in his pockets, watching her leave. There was a pulling feeling in her chest that didn't die down until they turned into the tunnel, and busy thoughts distracted her again.

"Here you are, at last! You should have been here before. I am worn ragged doing this charade myself. Get your apron, and come on."

Betty, panting with panic as usual, turned and huffed back inside. Danny rolled his eyes and winked at Martha as she stepped down.

It was a charade, Martha had to agree. The regal table was set for 14 people and 5 courses. Dust covers gone, curtains opened, candlesticks polished, it was an astounding room. The mahogany shine was covered with dinnerware, crammed with candles, but still, in Martha's eyes, barren. It took her a brief moment to identify why, and then she noticed it: there were no flowers, no holly leaves, and no signs whatsoever of the forest outside.

"Have we forgotten to gather decorations for the table?" she asked.

"There will be no berries or living things here. Mistress cannot abide it. And don't you say another word about it. Yours is not to question why."

Betty was defensive. The 40 years of service had built up a fortress of resignation, impenetrable to hope or change. In Betty, Martha saw another darkened, smothered place, and it saddened her.

"I'm sorry. So who are we expecting today?"

"We, my dear, are expecting no-one. The mistress is expecting one. The rest of the seats are a hankering after times long gone. They will not be filled by living people, only memories."

Martha felt a coldness whisper over her. "Who is the one?"

"The one? The one is the ever-wandering, ever-unreliable Lord Fitzgerald himself. Dear knows whether he'll be here - depends on his notions."

"But I thought he was-" Martha caught herself.

"Dead? Close your mouth child, you look foolish. No, he's not dead, though he might as well be, for all he's here. Our Lord Fitzgerald is a man of science. Wastes his time searching the earth for plants. Impossible man."

"But she -"

"Hates the things. Now you know why. It's nature that's brought her to this dark place, and nature that's taken her husband away from it. Leaving her on her own. With all she has had to bear. I've said enough now, too much. Don't you go repeating. And don't ask any more. For pity's sake, get back to work and stop holding that fork."

Martha started polishing again, her head filing away all that she had heard, her heart thudding with the terrifying idea of meeting her master. What kind of a man would he be. What kind of a husband would turn his wife into shadows. She knew she must wait and look without judgement. It was not her place. And yet, she felt that perhaps there was more need for her here than she had first thought.

After a day of flapping from Betty, and a fortune of fuss, the bell rang for dinner. The staff had barely time to shovel in a turkey sandwich when they were called to take their places, and the great charade began. Martha's place was to be on hand should her mistress make a whimsical demand, and so she stood in the shadows, waiting. The Lord and Lady came in separately, and took their places at the head of the table, looking down on a mass of detailed, empty places.

"Really, every year you're going to do this? What a waste, there's plenty of guests we could have had, if you'd only thought to ask."

Lord Fitzgerald was small, and rosily indignant. He pulled on his ear lobes, agitated. Martha looked at his protruding ears, and wondered why he encouraged them so. His face had been beaten by the heat of the Burmese sun and his eyes were faded with too much study, but with a hint of kindness about them. What remained of his hair was a web of black strings, plastered to his sweating head, tucked behind those ears. As he sat down, his coat tails flapped out, and reminded his silent observer of the blackbird that had made her mistress shriek. Well, Martha liked birds, and she found herself liking the master, whatever wrong turns he'd made.

"I need lemon in my water, girl!"
Martha rushed to the lady's command, and so revealed herself to the little man's scrutiny.

"How fascinating! What is that around your neck?" The Lord pointed, and leaned towards her.

Martha's hand flew up to the seed necklace Danny had made her, sorry that it had fallen out of hiding.

"It's nothing, just a gift from a friend. I beg your pardon."

"A truly wonderful gift, my dear. Do you know what they all are? You do? That's marvellous! Isn't it marvellous, darling?"

Lady Fitzgerald sighed, and took a sip of her water.

"This one shares your ridiculous fascination with nature, Henry. I, as you may remember, do not."

The meal went on in chinking, scraping silence after that. Now and again Martha's master would start to pull out a notebook, and then catch himself. Now and again he would glance towards Martha, looking as though he wanted to question her further. Lady Fitzgerald sat stubborn, and ate little.

It was the least happy Christmas Martha had ever known.

* * *

Martha only had one more occasion to see her master before he left again. She had been sent to clean the library – a room that she had never been in before. She opened the door to an unfamiliar but not unpleasant smell. The sunlight pushing in through semi-shuttered windows caught dancing particles of dust, and then was blocked with what lined the curved walls. Martha looked up and then around at shelf after shelf of books. They reached such a height that there was a ladder to get to the top. Realising that she would have to use it to dust, Martha put one foot on the first rung to test it. There was a crack. She jumped and stepped down.

"Don't worry, the ladder is quite safe. It was only me. I see you're intrigued by my books." The master was smiling, eyebrows up, waiting for a response.

"I am sorry, sir. I did not realise you would be in this room so early. I'll come back." Martha started backing out, when he beckoned her back.

"Would you like to see one – about wild

berries perhaps?"

"My reading is not very good, sir. But I would like that very much."

Martha looked over her shoulder, worried that Betty would catch her shirking.

"Don't worry about your chores - I will speak for you if anyone asks. This is an important task too - and it pleases me, so everyone wins."

The little man grinned, opened the book on indigenous trees, and beckoned Martha over.

And so it was that master and maid sat together, identifying the berries on Martha's necklace and looking at things of nature that enthralled them both – one in the mind, and one in the heart.

Chapter 7: Past Revealed

Not until we are completely lost, or turned around...do we appreci- ate the vastness and strangeness of Nature

Week pushed in after week, and the darkness of January bore down on everyone. Lord Fitzgerald had left shortly after Christmas, travelling with some fellow Botanists to look at and report a new discovery in eastern Asia. Every Sunday, Martha was surprised to be told that Lady Fitzgerald had requested that she accompany her to church. Now, the different worship rites were becoming familiar to her, and she began to forget how things were before, almost enjoying the difference. One Sunday, at the end of the month, the mistress shook her head to Martha, and went into the church alone. Puzzled, Martha stayed in the carriage, but left the door open. The wind was screaming and angry that day, but she was undaunted.

"Hello there. Want to come with your old friend to see this grave, and hear a story?"

There was Danny, poking his head through another door, looking wild with the weather, and almost rebellious.

"I'd never say no to fresh air, Danny. But is it alright? How would the mistress feel?"

"She'll never know. And anyway, she can't make a scene of walking up to it every week in front of your eyes, if she doesn't want you to know."

Martha made a dubious face, but got down. The pair set off, fighting the gale, and soon found themselves standing in front of a small headstone. The size of it pained Martha.

"Oh Danny, I don't think we should be

here. This is her private grief, we shouldn't step in on it."

Martha turned, and was starting to walk away, when Danny started speaking.

"She was only 8 years old. She shared her daddy's love of nature. Was always outside, exploring. One day she ran too far, maybe chasing after a bird, we'll never know. She was trying to climb up one of the biggest trees."

"We found her Martha, neck broken, beneath it. There was nothing to be done."

"That walk back to the house, carrying her, was the hardest thing I have ever known. The mistress was changed that day; all her light was gone, she shut it all out, and has never let anything in since. Her darkness, Martha, is her only companion.

"You are the first person, ten years on, that has made her turn to something else. I don't know why, but I am very glad of it."

Martha was kneeling now, tracing the letters on the stone, feeling the hard coldness of it, and the story it told.

"Best go back now, my dear."

Rubbing her sleeve over her cheeks, Martha took Danny's outstretched hand, and together they walked back. Reluctant to get back in the stuffy coach, Martha kept the door open, and sat on the step. She and Danny talked for a while about the little girl, and her mother's changed behaviour since that terrible day.

After what seemed like a short while, the mistress came out of the church, and saw them. She stopped, her face showing, only for an instant, that she knew what Martha had found out, and where they had been. Then, holding her head up, she swept past them, and climbed up into the blackened coach.

Lady Fitzgerald and Martha were silent the whole way back. Martha didn't dare to glance over, but kept her head down, allowing the sad thoughts to wash over her, and ebb away.

"In fact, I would like you to leave me

now."

Martha looked over, confused.

"I want to make the rest of the journey alone." Lady Fitzgerald banged the wall of the carriage and it came to a stop.

Danny opened the door, as confused as Martha.

"Martha is getting out now. We will go on without her."

Knowing not to question her mistress, Martha got down and watched the carriage pull away. It was a different lane to the one she had travelled before. She had never seen these sights, as it had always been in the blackened out windowless carriage. As she followed the narrow road, she looked all around her, marvelling at the beauty so willingly shut out by Lady Fitzgerald. The trees were deciduous, with silvery bark. The forest floor was twinkling with snowdrops, and fairy-tale toadstools.

Then, suddenly, she got the impression of more light and space. She stopped. There, metres away, was a shining lake. As though the trees had cleared a space for it, the water stood, mirror-like, reflecting back its thanks. It was like the forest was bowing to this scene. On the shimmering surface floated dozens of lily pads, green and pure. It was a still day, and apart from the whisper of trees, there was barely a sound.

Leaning against a boulder at the water's edge, Martha felt a deep peace coming to her, and all of a sudden, she knew that this silver, shining place was one of the hidden treasures Danny had promised her that first day. Water and sky, her two loves, had been here all along.

She pulled herself away from the lake, and, feeling drawn to see more, she turned off the flat, straight road to make her way up the slope on her left. The hill kept going, and there was no chance of Martha stopping, until a sight halted her. Just beside the path, there was a tree which her brothers would have said was 'made for climbing'. Standing right next to it, she tucked up her skirt, and lifted one leg up to the first branch. Getting the sap between her fingers, and feeling the tree moving in the breeze, Martha realised she had missed this - always being helmed in by walls, closed windows and obligations. She got up as far as she could, shifted herself so she was half-sitting on the fork of a large branch, and then she looked out: over the tops of the trees, across the fields, and then she saw a thin, tantalizing strip of blue water.

"So Danny was right - you can see the sea from here!"

Laughing to herself, she turned to look back at the tree. There, right next to her, were carved letters: 'G F'. They were faint, obviously having been there for some years. Martha traced them with her finger, and then realised they were the same letters she had gone over a few hours before. She knew who had done these ones. It was the daughter, the little girl who had died climbing trees just like this one.

"Oh God, it was this one, wasn't it?"

Quickly, Martha clambered down, ashamed of stepping on tragic memories. When she got to the bottom, she noticed a bunch of roses, tied to the back of the tree trunk.

"It wasn't me, dear, if that's what you're

thinking."

"Danny, what on earth are you doing here?"

"Wondered where you'd got to, then followed this flattened path, and here you are, climbing her tree."

"I didn't realise until I was up, and it was too late, I'm very sorry."

"Why? This is a tree made for climbing, not crying over. It's about time somebody put their hands and feet on it again. I'm glad it was you."

Chapter 8: The walled garden

Rise free from care before the dawn, and seek adventures.

Winter fought its way through to spring. Martha's tiny window was permanently covered with icicles, in and out. She couldn't remember what it felt like to be warm, or to see beyond the house. Her concerns for her family increased, as her thoughts of them became more and more unreal. Now and again, Danny would hand-deliver a letter from her mother, but the illiteracy of it would shed no light on what was really going on. As Martha's physical world closed in on her, her mind and spirit opened wider still.

57

She fed herself with recollections of her sea views, hopes for returning home, and of course, with her prayers. Sometimes, that is. Other times, it was simply too hard, and the loneliness won out.

Then, one day in April, Martha was given the rare gift of a free half hour. Bursting out the backdoor, she ran along the gravel, and down the drive.

"Today," she said to herself, "I am going to explore."

Knowing exactly where the adventure would take her, she directed her steps towards a wall. The wall with a door that she had been curious about since her first day. She pushed the bolt back, and shoved the door against long grass on the other side. When there was a gap wide enough, she squeezed through, and stopped.

Before her was a delightful chaos of spring. The flowers had defied winter, and many had opened early. There were no tidy flower beds, or neat rows: wild flowers were allowed the freedom to grow where they pleased, and live up to their name. There were some climbing up the red brick walls, fighting each other for the best space at the top. At the bottom, everything was overlapped, so it was difficult to make out which branch or stem belonged to which plant. Although there was confusion, it was a joyful chaos, unapologetic for its beautiful abandon. Martha picked her way on tiptoes through the colour, making a mental catalogue of all the plants she recognised from her own woods, and wondering at all those she did not. Looking down, she noticed a little one that she knew well, and, knowing that one wouldn't be missed, she picked it.

"Herb robert? Of course. That's the flower for you!"

Martha started, and turned.

"It's only me."
"So you've found my garden at last. Do you like it?"

Danny stood grinning, toothless, and swept his arm around the space.

"That's words enough, don't cry now. It's not really mine, I've just given it the breath it needed."

Danny looked away as Martha recovered her composure.

"Small, bright, a wee treasure in gloomy places - it's perfect for you Martha. You take that with you, and keep it to remind you there are still good things, even here."

"Anyway, I was sent to find you. I guessed your curiosity might have won out and brought you to the garden, and so, here I am. Mistress wants you."

Martha committed the scene to precious memory, and hurried back to the house, the little pink flower tucked safely up her sleeve.

Skirting round the staff dining room, she was stopped by the sound of laughter. It wasn't a kind sound, or cheerful. It was too loud, too harsh. Someone was shouting the same thing over and over, "Cat's got your tongue. Cat's got your tongue." Moving round to one of the doors, Martha saw a group of about ten servants circling around something. All of them were looking and laughing – some with their heads thrown back, some knowing they should feel more shame. All of a sudden the racket stopped, and Martha saw Danny pushing his way in, making the others step back. He got to the centre, and crouching down, pulled a boy to his feet. Taking him by the shoulders, he led him back past the benches, and out the door where Martha stood. The boy was younger than her, and his face made him more childlike still. His eyes were wide with bewilderment, and he kept turning his head from side to side. His worn trousers swung around his calves, and his shirt was buttoned haphazardly. Danny took his hand, and led him away, talking to him all the time.

Martha followed them out, and then hunkered down beside the wall, watching Danny calming the boy, and feeling bothered at the cruelty she'd just seen. She knew that many of the staff were not bad, by themselves, but together, they became monstrous. No wonder she hated the dining room, if things like this happened.

"His name is Pat. He's got a special way with him, that most don't understand."

Martha stood up, and waited as Danny poked the ground with his stick, digging for more words.

"I knew a Pat once. Still do."

"Where is he, Danny?"

Danny shook his head a few times,

"He's somewhere they say is safer for him, and everyone else. They think he is dangerous, but he's never harmed a soul. They took him away after the fire."

"Who did?"

"Our cousins. They didn't want him bringing disgrace on the family, but they had no room, so they took him to the Workhouse. I knew he couldn't come here, not without permission. But he didn't start it, Martha. He belonged with me, in our house, our parents' home. I couldn't fight them, they wouldn't have listened anyway. And now, every week that I see him, he's more full of shadows. He just sits there, in his workhouse clothes, like a prisoner. I know what he needs, Martha. He needs a chair with a sky view like yours. He's an angel on earth, and no-one looks at him enough to know that, you see. That's why I will always fight for Pat, and any like them. "

Martha opened her mouth to speak, but Danny had already turned away.

Martha didn't see Danny around the grounds for some time after that, and then when she passed him, he didn't look up at her, and seemed preoccupied. She went to the walled garden in the hope of speaking to him, but he was never there. She had never known, or asked, where he could be found after sunset when all the work was done.
One night, however, she woke to a repetitive tapping on her door. She sat up and listened.

"Martha! Martha!'

Martha got up from her lumpy mattress, pulled her shawl round her, and opened the door.

Danny was standing there, paraffin lamp in his hand, droplets of rainwater on his forehead, tears in his eyes.

"You have to help me, I've lost him, and

now I'm for it if I can't bring him back, and the mist is covering everything. He'll be frightened, and dear knows where he'll go."

"Who, Danny? Who will be frightened?"

"Just please come help me, I know you won't tell a soul."

Danny turned and started down the steps, with Martha behind him. When they got out, Martha saw that a thick wall of grey fog had surrounded the house, making it impossible to see more than an arm's length in front of them. Danny lit his lamp, and holding it high, started moving forwards.

"Wait, Danny. Do you know where he might have gone?"

Danny didn't answer, but just kept walking, counting his steps under his breath. They stumbled forward, first over the gravel in the courtyard, then sodden grass. The mist was so dense, that Martha began to lose sight of Danny, and had to follow the sound of his counting. Her foot dropped into holes in the uneven ground, and she felt the wet mud soak into her bedsocks, and only pair of shoes. All of a sudden, there was a new sound. At first, Martha thought that it was her calling out, but as it got closer, she realised it was a man's voice.

"Danny! Danny! Danny!" the voice sounded over and over.

"I'm coming Seamus, just stay where you are!"

Danny started to run, waving the light around him until the beams caught the glint of eyes not five feet away.

Martha caught up to the sight of Danny holding another man, and rubbing his hair, talking in soft tones all the while. The stranger was letting out loud sobs, and was stamping his feet. He didn't speak, just whimpered out Danny's name.

"Well Martha, this is my brother."

"But I thought-"

"I know. I couldn't bear it any longer, I discharged him from the workhouse and brought him here, to live with me. Mistress knows, but she warned me that any trouble, and he'd have to go back. So you can see, I had to find him."

"But why was he out alone, Danny? On a night like this?"

"I told him off for not putting his dish away, and he ran out."

On hearing this, Seamus started to groan again. He was a big man, strong muscled and tall. His size, combined with his strange sounds were frightening, but Martha stepped forward and took his hand.

"Hello, Seamus, I'm glad to meet you. Let's see if we can make our way back now."

Chapter 9: War breaks in

When summer was in full bloom, darkness found another way to steal in. Martha heard little of the outside world, and not much from her family. News about the war was basic, and seemed very remote from the inward-looking goings-on of the big house. Some of the staff talked about people they knew joining up, but it was too early, and the battlefields too far away for anyone to know anything in much detail. In some ways, the lack of knowing fed the fear and dread in Martha, but she let business push that aside.

One day, however, two things happened. Martha was cleaning near her mistress' room when the sound of raised voices and distress reached her. Not long after, she saw a man with a doctor's bag coming and going. Her master came out of the room at one point, and saw Martha standing there, but just looked down and did not speak as he passed her. There was a frightening uneasiness about the whole thing, but yet again, Martha was left to wonder.

She did not see Betty until the next day, holding a letter, looking unusually concerned.

"I have post for you. You had better prepare yourself."

Martha's legs began to shake. She took the page and read it.

Peter has gone to fight. He sends his farewell to you.

"It's taking many men, dear. Even your master. It's up to us women to be strong here now."

"I know it's a shock to you, living here in this locked up place."

Betty put her hand on Martha's back, and patted it a few times. Martha nodded her thanks, and then walked away, trying to hold herself steady. She climbed up the stairs to her room and fell to her knees. It was the first time she hadn't stood on her chair to find the sky.

Chapter 10: Letters to and from the Front.

Time is but the stream I go fishing in. Its thin current slides away, but eternity remains.

10th *November 1915*

Dear Martha, I am writing to you from the Front. It turns out that your master is now mine – he's been tasked with leading our division of the New Irish Army and a very fair captain he is too.

It is a very strange way of living here, but we all try to jolly ourselves along. The trenches are worse than the muddiest bogs at home - you have to just expect to have boots and socks full of muddy water! I

*miss our warm turf fires, and the chance of dry
clothes now. I'll not tell you about the rats, as I know
you hate them already.*

*It is hell here, Martha. Every day, when it's our
week to be in the frontline trench, we're ordered to
climb up over the top, and many never come back
alive. I've made and lost good friends - some from
machine gunfire, but mostly to the poisonous gas the
enemy attacks with. There are not enough gas masks
for everyone, and they're such a bother to get on in a
hurry, that it's sometimes too late. Don't worry - I'm
lucky enough to have one, but if I saw someone
struggling without, I'd like to think I would lay
down my life for them, and give them mine.*

*I do miss home, and all of you. The sea seems
like another world now. But I'm sure it won't be long
til this is over, and I'm back with you again. Please
send my love to mother, father and the wee ones. I
pray for them and you every night.
Peter.*

12th Feb 1916

*Dearest Peter, what a joy to get your letter – it
only arrived this morning. I am very glad you are
safe, and know that you can't tell very much. There*

71

are probably no words even if you could. It's good that Lord Fitzgerald is with you – and strangely comforting to think that we both share him now.

All the family, especially mother and father, were so relieved to hear from you. They wish you back with them every day.

I have very little news – it all seems so unimportant. I discovered a beautiful walled garden here last year. I wish you could see it. I haven't gone near since you left, perhaps I want to wait and save it for you. When you close your eyes in that dark, awful place, try and imagine walking in it with me. One day you will, I promise, Peter.

Keeping you in my prayers, and sending you all my love, Your Martha.

17th April 1916

Dear Martha, it's been a long time since I last wrote. A life-time I think. I hope this letter finds you and the family well. I wonder what season it will be when you read this. I have almost nothing I can tell you. I still try to pray, but it is very dark here. I wish

I could see more light.

Peter.

5th April 1916

Dear Peter, I don't know why I am writing to you now. But I feel like I need to. Maybe somehow you'll hear my words, I wish that would be true. They told me that you fought bravely, that you stood by your comrades. That you died a hero's death. Oh but I would exchange all that praise for you to come home again.

Mother is lost. I'm told that very evening, she climbs up the hill and looks as though she is waiting. Perhaps hoping that you will appear round the corner at any moment. My master has returned, and has lost his arm, and worst of all, his sight. Of course, to the mistress, he might as well be dead. She does not know how fortunate she is that the one she was waiting for has come back.

I have not had the chance to speak to him about you yet. I'm afraid I will not be able to hear it.

I have only one comfort. You wished for more

light, and now, you are in it.

I cannot wait to see you there, my dear.

Looking up from her writing at the bare floorboards in her cramped room, Martha tried to compose herself, but couldn't find peace, only rising, pounding panic. She stood up, feeling the close walls getting closer, the tiny square of daylight closing over, the air staler. She found herself stumbling back down the stairs, scraping her hands against the rough stone, nearly falling. Bursting out into the courtyard, she took deep breaths of the fresh air, and started to walk.

After a long while, her legs got heavy, her steps smaller, until she came to a stop. Finally lifting her head, she found she was on the edge of the forest, next to a field. She gasped, as she took in the sight that was before her: dozens of white geese were crying and flying in a V formation towards the grass. In small groups, and then in turn, they came to rest. Despite the clamour and commotion, it was in this moment that Martha found peace. She stood and watched the birds, so graceful in flight, then so clumsy on the ground, and loved them.

She did not see the two men walking steadily towards the geese. She did not see their guns. She did not see them raise their weapons, or point them. Two cracks burst into her consciousness. Then a terrible, high-pitched crying, and clapping of many wings pushed her face-first to the earth. She crawled to the wall, and looked over. The two hunters were retreating, one goose in each hand. Not all four were dead, however. There was one still moving, beating against the grip of his would-be killer. The fight for life was quickly ended when the man walked over to the wall, close to Martha, and cracked the bird's head against it.

Terrified, she crouched lower, and waited for them to leave. Once out of hearing, she began to weep – for the goose, for its companions. For Peter.

Chapter 11: Martha gets sick

This is a cold world

"What are you doing out in that weather? You're soaked right through. You'll have to go and change now, and there's still work to do. Honestly Martha, you should know better."

Martha stood, dripping and shivering, letting Betty work out her indignation.

"Well?"

"Lady Fitzgerald wanted me to check the stables. She's lost a hat-pin, and wants me to look for it. I've still to search the drive."

"Gracious! A hat-pin. She'll have you catch your death before she calls in all her riches. Dear, dear. I suppose you have to go out again, but that's the last of it. Check the drive, then come straight in."

So, Martha turned and faced the driving rain. It started to bite at her face, as it froze into hail. She could barely see as she tried to pick out the pin. Even if it was there, the pearl would be unrecognizable amongst the white clumps of ice. Eventually, she gave up, and went into the house. Betty was still standing there, waiting.

"Right, up you go to change. I will answer to the mistress. She's losing her mind stuck in this place, fretting over master."

Martha climbed the stairs, struggled off her soaking coat, dress, tights and undergarments. Cold to the bone, she pulled on dry clothes, and gathering the wet ones up, she went down again.

Her remaining chores were done in an aching blur. She couldn't manage her food, and was just on her way to lie down, when

Betty came to her again.

"I'm afraid mistress wants to hear it from you. Straight to bed after that, mind."

With heavy limbs, too cold to worry, Martha went to Lady Fitzgerald.

"So, you searched everywhere? The stables? The grounds? The stairs?"

Martha nodded.

"What am I going to do? This is a real loss. You will have to look again tomorrow."

"Yes, ma'am."

Concentrating on staying on her feet, Martha slowly left. She was nearly up the stairs to her own room when her legs gave way. With one last push, she made it to her bed, and gave up.

The night passed in a confusion of dreams and fever. Alone, Martha suffered. When morning came, she was no better, and nobody knew.

At some point, she heard the sound of

someone coming up her stairs.

"Oh my poor dear, I shouldn't have let you go out. I'll send one of the girls to look after you today."

Betty's face was above Martha, and had an unfamiliar kindness to it. Martha whispered her thanks, her sense of duty beaten down by sickness.

"This is a real loss". She lay and allowed the words of her mistress to wash over her, struggling with the angry bitterness they brought.

Chapter 12: Master encounters

The earth is not a mere fragment of dead history...but living poetry like the leaves of a tree

Life went on as usual in the isolated world of the big house. Her sickness passed, Martha welcomed the chores, working herself into a strange, care-free state. She did not take the breaks offered to her, she was afraid of the space to think, afraid of the terrible places her thoughts would take her. She knew Danny's garden would be in full colour, and that she was missing it. It would feel like a betrayal of Peter to go there, when he had spent his last days in the hell of the trenches. She had asked the other servants what they knew of the war, and even those few facts were more than she could bear. She thought of her mother and father, her other brothers and sisters, and needed to be with them. She began to resent the duty that kept her away, and avoided company. The house and all its incomprehensible goings-on were becoming a farce. Being away from reality had been tolerable before, but now it felt like a waste. Surely, Martha thought, she could be of more use somewhere else.

Once again, she found herself being given the task of dusting the library. Not expecting anyone to be there, she opened the heavy door, and stepped inside. As her eyes adjusted to the curtained darkness, she made out the bent figure of her master. He was sitting behind the desk, his remaining hand resting on the open book in front of him. His eyes were staring, but filled with tears. Martha made to back out of the room unnoticed.

"Martha? Is that you? Light footsteps – it must be you"

Martha walked towards the desk, caught.

"Yes, sir, it's me. I am sorry – I thought

the room would be empty."

"Empty because what could a blind man find of use in here, you mean. It is a mocking place to be, but somehow I find myself coming back to it all the time. I haven't seen you, I mean, I haven't been near you, since I came back."

"I am so sorry about Peter, Martha. He was a brave, good boy. You know, I actually owe my life to him. He gave me his mask, when I couldn't reach mine. Do you want me to tell you about it?"

"I don't think I want to hear about that yet, sir. But I am glad you knew him, and were with him there."

Martha wrung the duster in an attempt to control her shaking hands, but her body trembled in spite of herself. She put her hand on the desk as she turned to go, but found it clumsily gripped.

"We won't speak of it until you are ready, or never, if you don't wish it. Don't leave on my account. Work away, or...In fact, Martha, I wonder if you could help me. Do you have the time to, like before, that is, can you read a little?"

Martha nodded, caught herself, and said she would.

"Do you think you could try and read to me, from time to time? Or even, describe what the seasons are bringing to our forest?"

His face looked alive for the first time, and Martha knew she had to say yes.

"I don't know if I would be able to manage the fancy books that you have read, sir. But I will try, and I would be glad to tell you about what I see."

And so it was that Martha became her master's eyes. Every morning, after her first chores were done, she met Lord Fitzgerald in the library, picked a book at his request, and muddled her way through a few pages.

"Today, let's try some American writings. Have you ever heard of Thoreau's work, *Walden*?"

"I haven't. Of course."

"Well, now you have. I marked the phrases that made the greatest impression on me when I first read his work, and if you can find one or two, and remind me of them, it would benefit both of us, I think."

Martha located the book, and turned the thin pages until she found pencil marks. She laughed, then read:

How then, could I have a furnished house? I would rather sit in the open air, for no dust gathers on the grass.

"That's a good one for you! Turn over two pages and find another."

We now no longer camp as for a night, but have settled down on earth and forgotten heaven.

"That one, I think Martha, does not apply to you, with your tiny room, and your prayerful character."

"It's not as easy now to think of heaven, when there's such hell here. I'm not the saint you imagine I am."

"Understood. Let's move on to one more, and then I'll stop keeping you back - Betty is a formidable lady when you cross her, I know."

Guided by her master, Martha found another underlined section, and read it before she went back to work.

There can be no very black melancholy to him who lives in the midst of nature and has his senses still.

As she climbed the ladder to reach the highest bookshelves, Lord Fitzgerald spoke again,

"There also can be no very black melancholy when you are here, bringing light and sight to me, Martha, and I thank you for that. Two saviours in one family, who'd have thought it?"

At the end of that week, Betty took pity on Martha, and gave her a day to go home. Once again, Danny helped her onto the cart, and they set off.

Danny didn't break the silence, but sitting beside him comforted Martha, and she was relieved not to have to manage open sympathy.

"You know," Danny said at last, "it's been a long time since I walked on the shore below your house. Would you mind showing me again today?"

"Oh Danny, I'd love to."

They reached the field before the family's rented cottage, and got down. It was a steep hill, but Martha led the way, half-running, half-stumbling until she reached the wooden stile. She looked back at Danny, puffing behind her, but now that she'd seen the sand she was restless to get down to it. She looked at the still estuary, and then closed her eyes to take in the sounds of a high tide lapping against the sloping rocks, the curlews crying, the trees creaking in the woods beside her.

"Well, are we climbing over or not?"

Martha jumped, and turned, remembering she wasn't by herself. The pair of them climbed the stile, jumped down the sand dune, and stopped themselves before they reached the water. There wasn't enough room to walk further, without clambering from one lump of bent to another. The water was moving with the tide, but its surface was almost unbroken, reflecting the forest behind it, and the motionless white clouds above.

"Look!" Danny whispered "A seal!"

They both stood still, and watched the black head moving towards them until it disappeared.

"This is what heaven's like, Danny. I'm sure of it."

Danny squeezed Martha's shoulder in agreement.

"Well, life on earth beckons, wee Martha, so we'd best get you to where you're needed most."

Danny left Martha at her gate, and drove away. She held onto it for a moment, praying for a strength she didn't trust herself to have, and then walked down to her family. Her mother was already out, standing at the half-door, watching and waiting. It seemed to Martha that this was where she was every moment she could be – looking for the son she'd lost but couldn't bury.

She reached out to her, and the two held onto each other for a long time. There were no words to grab hold of all the grief they were living, and so they said nothing.

Chapter 13: A confrontation

we can stand aloof from actions and their consequences and all things, good and bad, go by us like a torrent

"Well, well, you're wanted by herself yet again, Martha. Pinch your cheeks and push up a more pleasant face - only the mistress is allowed to look so heartbroken."

Ever sensitive, Betty led the way to Lady Fitzgerald. Martha straightened her apron, pushed her hair back into its pony-tail, and tried not to feel. Walking up the long corridor like she had done on her very first day, she was no longer intimidated. She had seen enough behind the pomp to know the frailty it tried to disguise.

"Martha!"

The mistress stood up and hurried towards her little servant, hands outstretched. Martha looked at them, at the altered figure, and felt pity. She dared to meet her mistress' eyes, and saw something in them she recognized.

"I cannot bear it. He has lost too much, he is not the man he was. I can barely look at him. He might as well be - "

"Dead? Is that what you were going to say? I am sorry, but it is a sin to wish that. I tell you, I would give anything to be able to have my brother here, to see him walk back to my family. But he is gone. He is dead. Never to come back on this earth, only leaving pain and emptiness. Your husband is still here. He's sitting down there alone, and you are here, alone, feeling sorry for yourself."

Martha caught herself, and stepped back, hand over her mouth. As she retreated she looked at Lady Fitzgerald's shock, then turned and rushed out of the room.

Speaking her mind, after months of holding back, did not bring the release that Martha had expected. She had felt exhilarated in the moment, but immediately afterwards, it was shame that worked at her.

"What have you been up to – running out of the mistress' room like that?"

Betty frowned, and took up her usual interrogative stance, hands on hips, chin pointing like a finger.

"I was just with Lady Fitzgerald, and now I am going back to my work."

Shaking her head, Betty moved on, and Martha put her hand against the wall to steady her pounding.

She worked in a fury, not seeing what she was doing, just feeling the dull thud of what she had done. She knew that all she had said was true, but it was not her place to challenge anything here. It was so hard, pushing all the grief into the background, and being only a servant, whose feelings were not to be considered. The master cared though, and that was something.

Chapter 14: Salvation

the sun shines bright and warm this first spring morning, re-creating the world.

There was silence from upstairs, until Sunday, when Martha was surprised to find her presence requested.

She shifted from one booted foot to another in her church clothes, waiting for the blacked out carriage. But the one that pulled up had windows, brightly open. She could see her mistress, and her master. Danny opened the door for her, shrugging his shoulders, and she climbed in.

"Good morning Martha. Do you like the carriage?"

"Yes, sir, I do. I will try and take in what I see, to tell you."

"Oh, it wasn't my idea, it was my wife's. She tells me she's not wearing black today either."

Lady Fitzgerald put her head down, pleased.

"Yes, you do look very well, ma'am." Martha avoided her mistress' eyes.

The coach journey was a joy to her – she took in the green of the forest, the glimmers of colour in the wild flowers at its foot, and the bright snatches of sky. At every discovery, she described what she saw to her master, and watched his face concentrate in the effort to imagine it all. All the while, Lady Fitzgerald kept glancing over at her.

When they stepped down from the carriage, they gestured for Martha to follow, and all three walked across the graveyard this time.

"I know you know, Martha. I saw Danny telling you something here a while ago. Thank-you for not mentioning it to me, to us."

Lord Fitzgerald jerked his head towards his wife, surprised.

"And you didn't mind?"

"Be calm, Henry – I am trying now."

Henry bent his head, and Martha saw his hand grip his stick until his knuckles were white. He cleared his throat.

"So, this is – was – our precious little girl. She would be the same age as you now, if she'd lived. Sometimes, I see a reflection of her in you, Martha."

"It's almost as though God sent you to be a light to us in this black grief."

Overwhelmed, the young girl looked down, and then her mistress stretched out her hand to her, just as Martha had done a long time before.

"You are our glimpse of sky, Martha."

The three, now united through shared grief, made their way back from the grave, knowing that life now would be different. Faced together, it would be better.

Chapter 15: Beginnings

There is more day to dawn. The sun is but a morning star.

After the open carriage, things were very different at the big house. Martha carried on with her usual tasks, but was unexpectedly interrupted from time to time, either by her master and his requests for things to be read to him, or, most unusually, by her mistress. She would follow her, pester her for trivial things, and mainly show a new, bright, curious side to her character. She got Martha to take her to Danny's garden, and marvelled at not ever being interested in it before. She climbed up to Martha's room, and even stood up on the chair to look out - knowing the rumours of a possible sea view from there. Of course she didn't see it, and Martha was not ready to tell her about the view from her daughter's tree.

From daybreak one sunny morning, the buzz in the servants' quarters, and the hubbub with horses, carriages and stable boys in the drive proclaimed happy news: a picnic by the sea. Betty was rosily flustered, the staff were all doing their best to avoid a tongue-lashing, but were so excited they would have borne it. After a flurry of washing apples and berries, cutting sandwiches and fruit cake and stacking crockery, it was ready.

Betty caught Martha frowning at the quantity of food, and, for the first time, she roared with laughter.

"Don't worry, my dear. There are real guests this time, not like Christmas. And, d'you know who they are?"

Martha shook her head: nothing would surprise her now. Betty grabbed Martha's arms, still smiling.

"It's us! Right down to the youngest girl in the kitchen, the smallest boy on the grounds, even Danny's brother. But the guest of honour is my own nephew, David, just home from the front."

Betty almost skipped away, much to Martha's silent consternation. All of the house staff and residents climbed up onto their respective carts or carriages, and they were off. The destination was a beach Martha had never been to, and as the horses bounced on, her anticipation grew. She looked around her, taking in the mountains graciously giving way to more gentle hillsides, the fields of sheep, displaying that immaculate painting of white and black on green, the carefully built stone walls, and the fuschia bushes lining the road. They climbed up a steep hill, and at the summit, looked down on the vast blue of the ocean, framed on both sides with grey rocks, and underlined by a golden shore. The sea was calm, but waves still broke in a white foam, genuflecting to their spectators - both servants and masters - making all equal in the face of their unparalleled majesty.

Everybody slowly got down, and, uncertain of the protocol, stood waiting for their superiors to lead the way. Hand in hand, Lord and Lady Fitzgerald walked down to the sand, and then, bending down, Lady Fitzgerald took her shoes off and picked her way over the sand, stockings still on, down to the water's edge.

There was an awkward pause, and then, one by one, the household staff followed suit. Martha stood, laughing, and watched the frivolity.

"You not going to dip your toe in too, Martha?"

Martha turned to see a man taller than her, but not much older, and looked into his familiar face.

"Oh, so *you're* David! You worked here before the war,"

"I wasn't sure you'd noticed. I, on the other hand, always noticed you."

David looked down, half mumbling the last sentence, while Martha, embarrassed, glanced over to the paddling people, hoping for a distraction.

"I'm sorry, I don't really understand. I've always kept myself to myself here, you know."

"But I always saw you - your dedication to the mistress, your shyness when you went into the dining room that time, you sneaking off to Danny's garden, and your desire for light and fresh air. Your true spirit."

"And then you left to fight. And now you're back, safe and well."

Martha changed the subject, hoping to wrap up the uncomfortable and unexpected praise David was so keen to give.

"You must think more of yourself, I could help you with that, if you'd let me. Would you let me?"

David's face was flushed. Martha, with a mixture of politeness and a glimmer of something much better, smiled, and slowly nodded her head.

"Well then, now will you come down to the water with me?"

David stretched out his hand, wee Martha

took it, and together, under a light-filled sky,
they ran to the sea.

L - #0229 - 010719 - C0 - 175/108/5 - PB - DID2553571